Sadie
the Saxophone
Fairy

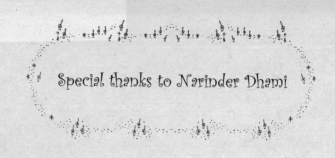

Special thanks to Narinder Dhami

ISBN: 978-0-545-10630-6

Copyright © 2008 by Rainbow Magic Limited.

All rights reserved. Published by Scholastic Inc., 557 Broadway, New York, NY 10012, by arrangement with Rainbow Magic Limited.

12 11 10 9 8 7 6 5 4 3   10 11 12 13 14 15/0

Printed in the U.S.A.

First Scholastic Printing, January 2010

Sadie
the Saxophone
Fairy

by Daisy Meadows

SCHOLASTIC INC.

New York Toronto London Auckland
Sydney Mexico City New Delhi Hong Kong

The Fairyland Palace

Ban

Wetherbury College

MALL
MEGA BIG NATURE

New Harmony Mall

The Village Hall

The Warehouse

Willow Hill

I'm through with frost, ice, and snow.
To the human world I must go!
I'll form my cool Gobolicious Band.
Magical instruments will lend a hand.

With these instruments, I'll go far.
Frosty Jack, a superstar.
I'll steal music's harmony and its fun.
Watch out, world, I'll be number one!

Contents

The Competition Begins   1

Green Factory   11

Ice Rap   21

I'm a Celebrity!   35

Shiny Saxophone   45

First Place Goes to…   55

The Competition Begins

"We'd better hurry, Kirsty," Rachel Walker said to her best friend, Kirsty Tate, as they jumped out of the car. "The talent competition is going to start soon!"

The girls waved at Mrs. Tate, who had just dropped them off. Then they hurried into the New Harmony Mall.

"Good afternoon, everyone," said a voice over the loudspeaker system as the girls went inside. "The auditions for the National Talent Competition are about to start, so please make your way to the north end of the mall."

Rachel and Kirsty glanced at each other as they wove their way through the crowd.

"There are lots of people here," Kirsty said anxiously. "I hope we find Sadie's magic saxophone before Frosty and his Gobolicious Band take the stage!"

The girls had been asked by their friends, the Music Fairies, to help them find their seven magic musical instruments, which had been stolen from Fairyland's Royal School of Music by Jack Frost and his goblins. The instruments were very important — they made music joyful and harmonious for everyone in both the human and fairy worlds. Since the instruments had gone missing, music everywhere had been ruined!

But Jack Frost had his own plans for the magic instruments. Along with his goblins, he had formed a pop group called Frosty and his Gobolicious Band. He intended to use the instruments' magical powers to win first place in the National Talent Competition. Rachel and Kirsty had managed to return six of the instruments to Fairyland, but they were still looking for Sadie's saxophone. Time was running out!

"I'm *so* worried that Jack Frost and the goblins are going to win the competition," Rachel confided to Kirsty as they hurried toward the stage at one

end of the mall. "If Frosty and his Gobolicious Band win the recording contract with MegaBig Records, it won't be long before *everyone* finds out about the existence of Fairyland!"

"I know," Kirsty agreed. "And even though Jack Frost only has one of the magic instruments left, its magic is so powerful that he could still win the competition!" At that moment, a man wearing a snazzy suit came onstage to loud applause.

"Good afternoon, and welcome to the first round of the National Talent Competition," he announced. "We have some fantastic acts for you to enjoy. Our judges will select the best four, and those acts will go on to this afternoon's LIVE, televised show!"

There were whoops of excitement from the audience.

"The first band to perform is Green Factory," the emcee went on. "While

they get ready, let me introduce you to
our distinguished judges . . . ."

"Green Factory!"
Kirsty whispered
to Rachel with
excitement.
"That sounds
like the perfect
name for a
goblin band!"
"Maybe Jack
Frost changed the
name from Frosty and his Gobolicious
Band so we wouldn't recognize it,"
Rachel suggested. "Let's get a closer
look at Green Factory, Kirsty!"

The girls tried to edge their way closer
to the stage, but there were so many

people that they didn't get very far. They
had to stand on tiptoe to look over the
heads of the crowd in front of them.
Then they could only catch glimpses of
Green Factory at the side of the stage,
tuning up their instruments.

"They're all very short, Rachel,"
Kirsty pointed out. "*And* they're dressed
in green!"

Rachel nodded. The band members were wearing emerald-green pants, T-shirts, and baseball caps.

"Remember how Jack Frost cast a spell to make his goblins the size of boys and take the green out of their skin?" Rachel whispered. "The Green Factory musicians look *exactly* the right size to be goblins!"

"I spotted something else, too!" Kirsty gasped. She pointed to where the stage lights were shining on a bright gold musical instrument. "Rachel, they have a saxophone!"

Green Factory

"So Green Factory *could* be Jack Frost's band!" Rachel exclaimed.

"Let's go backstage," Kirsty suggested. "We may be able to find Sadie's saxophone before Green Factory performs!"

The girls rushed backstage. There were lots of people milling around, so no one noticed Rachel and Kirsty slip into the wings.

"Now what?" Rachel whispered.

Kirsty was staring closely at the members of Green Factory. "Rachel, they aren't goblins!" she exclaimed. "The person with the saxophone is Courtney Lewis — she's my friend from school!"

"Oh!" Rachel looked disappointed. "I really thought we'd found Sadie's saxophone!"

Just then, Courtney glanced over. She looked upset, but smiled when she spotted Kirsty.

"Hey," Courtney called. "What are you doing here, Kirsty?"

"We came to wish you good luck," Kirsty replied, thinking fast. "This is my friend Rachel."

"Hello." Courtney smiled at Rachel. "Meet the rest of Green Factory — Katie, Jess, Molly, and Emma."

The girls grinned at Rachel and Kirsty.

"Are you nervous about performing

today, Courtney?" Kirsty asked. "You looked a little upset."

"Well, I've been practicing really hard, but my saxophone sounds *awful*!" Courtney sighed. "I don't know what's wrong with it."

Rachel and Kirsty shared a secret glance. They knew exactly why Courtney's saxophone didn't sound right. It was because Jack Frost still had the last magic musical instrument — the saxophone!

"We're cutting my sax solo from our performance," Courtney went on. "I'm the lead singer, so I'll still get to perform, but we won't have a chance of winning if I play my

saxophone. The audience would
definitely try to plug their ears!"

"And now for our first band," called
the emcee. "It's Green Factory!"

"Here we go!" Courtney held her
saxophone out to Kirsty. "Would you
hold this for me until we're finished?"

Kirsty nodded,
taking the
saxophone.

"Good luck!"
she and Rachel
said together.

Courtney and
the other girls
hurried to the
center of the

stage. Rachel and Kirsty slipped out of
the wings and rejoined the audience just

as Green Factory launched into their song, "School Days."

"This is great!" Rachel said enthusiastically to Kirsty after the first few bars.

"I never realized Courtney was so talented!" Kirsty replied.

"It's lucky the other six instruments are back in Fairyland," Rachel added. "It means that music everywhere is almost

 back to normal now, so Green Factory's talent can still shine through!" The band finished their song, and the audience

cheered loudly. The Green Factory
musicians took a bow and then hurried
into the stage wings. Rachel was still
applauding, but Kirsty was staring
down at Courtney's saxophone,
looking puzzled.

"Rachel!" Kirsty nudged her friend as
the emcee announced the next band.
"Look at the saxophone!"

Rachel glanced down. To her
amazement, the shiny golden sax was

bouncing around in Kirsty's hands as if it had a life of its own!

"It's like magic!" Rachel said, in complete awe. "It *can't* be Sadie's saxophone. Courtney said it sounded awful, and the magic instruments always play beautifully!"

Kirsty peeked into the open end of the saxophone.

"Rachel, I can see glitter!" she whispered.

Rachel peeked in, too. There was a tiny burst of dazzling glitter inside the saxophone!

"It's me, girls," said a small voice. "Sadie the Saxophone Fairy!"

Kirsty and Rachel grinned at each other. Quickly, they moved away from the crowd and hid behind a display of tall plants in clay pots.

"You can come out now, Sadie!" Rachel whispered. "It's safe."

Immediately, Sadie the Saxophone Fairy burst out of the saxophone in a mist of pale blue sparkles!

Ice Rap

"Oh, girls! Jack Frost is here at the competition!" Sadie cried, floating down to land on Kirsty's shoulder. She wore a green-and-blue ruffled dress with a glittery sweater around her shoulders, sparkly blue knee-high boots, and a matching headband. "We *have* to stop him from winning first place. Everyone in Fairyland is depending on us!"

"We'll do our best, Sadie!" Rachel assured her.

"I'd better give Courtney her saxophone back first," Kirsty said.

Sadie zoomed into Kirsty's pocket and the girls hurried backstage to find Courtney. She and her band were busy packing their instruments away.

"Green Factory was great, Courtney!" Kirsty said, handing over the saxophone.

"You'll definitely make it to the finals," Rachel added.

"Oh, I hope so!" Courtney replied.
"See you later. Thanks for holding on to
my saxophone!"

"We'd better go and look for Frosty
and his Gobolicious Band!" Kirsty
whispered to Rachel as Courtney and
the rest of Green Factory headed off
to the dressing room area.

The girls hurried back to the audience.
The band that had performed after
Green Factory, a group of four teenage
girls, was just finishing its song.

"We haven't seen any goblins at all
yet," Rachel remarked. "There weren't
even any backstage."

"They're probably hiding so we don't
have a chance of getting Sadie's
saxophone back!" Kirsty replied.

The next performer was a rock group.

They were followed by six other bands, performing songs ranging from hip-hop to jazz. But there was no sign at all of Frosty and his Gobolicious Band. Sadie and the girls couldn't understand it.

"Where are Jack Frost and the goblins?" Sadie whispered, peeking over the top of Kirsty's pocket. "Thank you, Red Socks!" the emcee announced as the jazz band left the stage. "We're coming to the end of the show now. If any other bands would like to take part, you'll have to act fast. The auditions will be closed after the next act!"

"This has to be Jack Frost," Rachel murmured to Kirsty.

"Now for our final band before we find out which lucky four will perform in tonight's live show," the emcee said with a smile. "Please welcome — Mountain Snow!"

Rachel, Kirsty, and Sadie watched eagerly, expecting to see Jack Frost and his goblins appear onstage. But they were surprised when a trio of older ladies walked out and began to yodel a pop song.

"They definitely aren't goblins!"
Rachel whispered, confused.

"Maybe Jack Frost decided not to enter
the competition at all after losing the
other six magic instruments," Kirsty
suggested.

"Then how will I ever find my
saxophone?" Sadie sighed.

The yodeling song finished, and the
crowd began to murmur in anticipation
of hearing the winners
be announced.
But suddenly,
the emcee rushed
onstage again.
"Ladies and
gentlemen, we
have a last-minute
entry!" he shouted.

"I'm happy to introduce — Frosty and his Gobolicious Band!"

Rachel gasped. "So Jack Frost and his goblins *are* here!"

Jack Frost strutted onto the stage, waving at the audience. He was accompanied by a group of twelve grinning goblins.

"Look at the goblin at the end of the line!" Sadie said excitedly.

The girls saw that the last goblin was holding a golden saxophone. The saxophone was the only instrument onstage, and it seemed to give off a magical shimmer.

"That's *mine*!" Sadie shouted, but her words were completely drowned out as

Jack Frost picked up the microphone. The crowd broke into spontaneous applause. "Hey, that lead singer's wearing such a cool costume!" said a boy standing next to Rachel.

"Yeah, all those fake icicles look awesome!" his friend agreed.

"Listen up!" shouted Jack Frost. He launched into a rap as the saxophone goblin began to play.

"I'm Jack Frost
And you'd better know
That I'm the king
Of ice and snow.
Don't mess with me
You'd better be nice,
Or I'll zap you with
My wand of ice!"

Rachel, Kirsty, and Sadie couldn't believe their ears. The saxophonist goblin was playing his heart out, and his catchy tune, swooping from high to low, somehow matched perfectly with Jack Frost's rapping. The goblins had divided into two groups — one group was performing backup vocals while the others were clapping, whistling, and snapping their fingers in time to the music.

"Jack Frost and the goblins sound amazing!" Rachel whispered to Kirsty.

The audience thought so, too. When Jack Frost finished his rap, they burst into thunderous applause. Looking smug, Jack Frost and his goblins took a sweeping bow. As they went off into the wings, Jack Frost waved graciously at the audience.

"What are we going to do?" Sadie asked the girls anxiously. "Frosty and his Gobolicious Band are sure to be finalists if the audience's reaction is anything to go by!"

"Here's the emcee to announce the

results," said Kirsty. "I guess we just have to see what happens."

The emcee had been talking with the judges, but now he was back onstage again.

"I can now announce the four finalists for tonight's show!" he began, beaming broadly. "The first band to go to the finals is . . . Green Factory!"

"Oh, good!" Kirsty exclaimed. "I'm so happy for Courtney."

"And our next finalist —" The emcee paused for a moment. "Frosty and his Gobolicious Band!"

This time the audience clapped even more loudly. Rachel, Kirsty, and Sadie looked at each other in dismay.

"Everyone loves Jack Frost and his goblins!" Rachel exclaimed. "They must be the favorite to win the competition tonight!"

Sadie nodded. "And the only way we can stop him," she said solemnly, "is to get my saxophone back before the finals!"

I'm a Celebrity!

Sadie ducked out of sight into Kirsty's pocket again, and the girls immediately rushed backstage to find the goblin with the saxophone. But when they arrived, they were frustrated to see a large group of people crowded around Jack Frost. Everyone wanted his autograph!

"One at a time, please!" Jack Frost was saying loudly.

"Jack Frost is already acting like a star, and he hasn't even won the competition yet!" Rachel murmured.

"There's Sadie's saxophone!" Kirsty whispered suddenly.

The saxophone-playing goblin was polishing the instrument with a cloth.

As the girls watched, he carefully put it away in its case. "Let's get a little closer to him," Rachel murmured. "But we have to be careful. We don't want Jack Frost or the goblins to recognize us!"

The girls began edging their way toward the goblin with the saxophone.

"I have to go to my dressing room and rest now," Jack Frost announced suddenly. "It's hard work being famous!"

He pointed to the tallest goblin.

"Keep an eye out for pesky girls and fairies!" Jack Frost ordered. "We can't risk losing the magic saxophone now. We need it for the finals."

The tall goblin nodded.

"Now let's go," Jack Frost snapped. Immediately, the other goblins cleared a path through the crowd. Jack Frost and the saxophone goblin swept through. "Don't let them get away, girls!" Sadie whispered. Rachel and Kirsty followed Jack Frost and the goblins toward the dressing rooms, but they had to keep their distance. The tall goblin kept looking around suspiciously.

"Get me something to eat and drink," Jack Frost demanded as they reached his dressing room. "Being a celebrity is hot and hungry work!" He grabbed the saxophone case from the goblin and marched inside, slamming the door behind him.

The girls watched as the goblins ran off to do Jack Frost's bidding. Meanwhile, the tallest goblin stationed himself outside the dressing room door.

"We have to find a way into that dressing room!" Kirsty whispered.

"But how are we going to get past the goblin bodyguard?" Rachel asked.

"Hello! Are you girls part of the makeup team?" said a voice behind them.

Rachel and Kirsty turned and saw three

teenage girls. They were carrying large
wicker baskets full of beauty products!

"Um — yes," Rachel blurted out,
glancing at Kirsty. What a perfect
way to get into Jack Frost's dressing
room!

"Oh, great," said one of the girls
gratefully, handing Rachel a basket.
"Is there a particular act you'd like to
work with?"

"Frosty and his Gobolicious Band!"
Kirsty and Rachel said eagerly.

The three girls laughed.

"You'd better get started, then," one of the others remarked. "From the looks of that band, their makeup might take a while!"

"Good thinking, Rachel!" Sadie whispered, as the three girls walked away. She fluttered out of Kirsty's pocket and quickly dove into the basket, hiding among the containers of makeup. "I'll try to grab my saxophone if I get the chance!"

Rachel and Kirsty hurried over to the goblin bodyguard at the dressing room door.

"We're here to do Jack Frost's makeup," Kirsty explained.

The bodyguard stared at them suspiciously for a moment.

"OK," he scowled, opening the door.
"But no monkey business!"

With that, Rachel and Kirsty went
inside. Jack Frost was sitting at the
dressing table, staring at his reflection
in an illuminated mirror. The open
saxophone case was on a table at the side
of the room. The golden instrument
glinted in the bright lights.

"What do *you* want?" Jack Frost
snapped.

"We're here to do your makeup,"
Rachel said quickly.

"We'll make you look like a star!"
Kirsty added.

Jack Frost smirked. "I like the sound of
that!" he said.

Rachel put the basket of beauty
products on the table next to the

instrument case. Sadie
peeked out and
grinned, spotting her
saxophone nearby.

"Let's start with your
hair," Rachel said,
grabbing a tube of
hair gel.

She and Kirsty
began applying gel to
Jack Frost's icicles, making them stand up
straight. The whole time, Jack Frost
admired himself in the mirror.

Kirsty glanced over her shoulder. Sadie
had managed to sneak silently out of the
makeup basket and was hovering above
her saxophone.

But just then, the door burst open —
and the goblins charged in!

Shiny Saxophone

"It's not fair!" one of the goblins roared. "*I* want to play the saxophone next time!"

"No, it's my turn!" yelled another.

"SILENCE!" Jack Frost shouted.

The goblins immediately went quiet.

"The goblin who played today is the ONLY one who's allowed to touch the saxophone," Jack Frost snapped. "That's because he is the ONLY goblin who has managed to hang on to his magic musical instrument!"

The other goblins hung their heads in shame. Meanwhile, Jack Frost turned to the saxophone-playing goblin.

"Make sure you polish the magic saxophone before the finals tonight," he ordered loudly. "I want it to look nice and shiny!"

Kirsty and Rachel glanced at each other. "It's a good thing that *we're* the makeup girls who are here," Kirsty whispered. "What would the other girls think, hearing Jack Frost talking about magic?"

"He obviously doesn't care about keeping Fairyland a secret at all!" Rachel replied.

One of the goblins rushed forward to hand Jack Frost the drink he had requested, but his boss waved him away impatiently.

"I'm not hungry or thirsty anymore," Jack Frost said with an air of importance. "I'm going to meet my fans and sign more autographs!"

Jack Frost strutted out of the dressing room, his goblins scampering after him. Only the saxophone player stayed behind. He took the instrument out of the case. Sitting down at the dressing table, he began polishing it again.

"Any ideas, girls?" Sadie whispered as Kirsty and Rachel pretended to organize the makeup basket. "Is there any way we can get my saxophone?"

"I don't think the goblin is going to put it down any time soon," Rachel said under her breath. "He's polishing so hard, he'll make it disappear if he's not careful!"

Kirsty grinned. "You just gave me an idea!" she exclaimed. "Sadie, could you use your magic to create a polishing cloth that will make the saxophone invisible? Then we might be able to get it away from him!"

"I sure can!" Sadie agreed. She twirled her wand, and a glittery pink cloth appeared in a cloud of fairy sparkles.

"You switch the cloths, Kirsty," Rachel whispered, as Sadie jumped into Kirsty's pocket. "I'll distract the goblin by doing his makeup!"

The goblin was still busy polishing, but he looked up suspiciously as Rachel went over to him.

"I'm here to do your makeup," she announced.

The goblin looked pleased. He put the cloth down, but held onto the saxophone.

Rachel opened a box of face powder and began to dab it onto the goblin's face with a big pad.

"Oh, that tickles!" The goblin laughed as he was surrounded by a cloud of white powder.

Meanwhile, Kirsty crept over, whisked away the polishing cloth, and put the magic one in its place.

"Hey!" The goblin blinked at her through the mist of powder. "What are you doing?"

"I thought you might like a clean cloth," Kirsty said quickly. "Look, some powder spilled onto your saxophone."

The goblin grabbed the magic cloth, laid the saxophone on his lap, and began polishing. Kirsty, Rachel, and Sadie watched eagerly.

"Jack Frost thinks he's the star of the band, but I'm the *real* star!" the goblin boasted.

Kirsty nudged Rachel as the mouthpiece of the saxophone began to disappear. But the goblin was too busy bragging to notice. Within seconds, the entire instrument had vanished!

Suddenly, the door flew open and Jack Frost and his goblins burst in.

"Why are you girls still here?" Jack Frost demanded furiously. "Get out! We need time to practice before tonight!" He glanced at the empty music case, then at the goblin sitting at the dressing table. "Where's the magic saxophone?"

The goblin looked down — and his eyes almost popped out of his head.

"It was here a minute ago," he mumbled, jumping up.

"Ow!" Jack Frost roared. "Something just fell on my foot!"

"The invisible saxophone!" Rachel whispered to Kirsty. The girls tried hard not to laugh.

As Jack Frost yelled at the goblin, Kirsty quietly bent down and felt around on the floor. Her hand closed over the invisible instrument.

"Someone stole the saxophone!" Jack Frost yelled.

He glanced suspiciously at Rachel and Kirsty, but, of course, he couldn't see the saxophone in Kirsty's hand at all!

"Find the magic saxophone!" Jack Frost shouted at his goblins. "Or our performance in the finals will be ruined!"

With that, they all dashed out of the dressing room again.

Immediately, Sadie zoomed over to the girls.

"Great work, you two!" She laughed, waving her wand over Kirsty's hand. The golden saxophone instantly appeared in a swirl of fairy dust, shrinking down to its Fairyland size.

"Thank you so —" Sadie began, clutching her saxophone tightly.

But all of a sudden, an ice bolt whizzed straight past their heads!

Rachel, Kirsty, and Sadie turned to see a furious Jack Frost standing in the doorway!

First Prize Goes to . . .

"Give me that saxophone!" Jack Frost shouted, preparing to aim another ice bolt.

Quickly, Sadie flicked her wand at Rachel and Kirsty. The magical sparkles surrounded the girls and instantly reduced them to fairy size. Then Sadie's magic whisked them straight off to Fairyland, just as another ice bolt flew across the room toward them!

Rachel gasped. "That was close!"

A few seconds later, the three friends landed on the stage in the Fairyland Royal School of Music to cheers and applause. King Oberon, Queen Titania, and the six other Music Fairies were waiting for them.

Royal School of Music

"You have the magic saxophone!" Queen Titania said, beaming with delight. "We knew you wouldn't let us down!"

"You have saved music everywhere!" King Oberon announced. "And now we will have a wonderful show to celebrate the return of the magic instruments. Thank you, girls!"

He stepped forward and handed Rachel and Kirsty two small golden boxes. The boxes shimmered with fairy magic.

"They are magical music boxes," the king

explained with a smile. "They'll play all your favorite fairy music whenever you like!"

Rachel and Kirsty beamed at each other. "Thank you!" they cried.

"Will you stay for our musical celebration?" Queen Titania asked.

"Thank you, but I think we'd better go back and watch the finals of the talent competition," Rachel replied.

"What about Jack Frost?" Kirsty asked anxiously. "Do you think his band might still win tonight, even without the magic instruments?"

"Don't worry!" Queen Titania laughed. "Without the instruments, the truth about Jack Frost's musical talent will be revealed!"

"Good-bye!" the girls called as the queen lifted her wand to send them back home.

"Good-bye, and thank you!" the Music Fairies chorused.

Rachel and Kirsty felt themselves spinning away in a whirl of magic, with sweet fairy music tinkling in their ears. A few seconds later, they were back in the mall and were normal girls once again.

"Please welcome back the fantastic Green Factory!" the emcee was saying.

"Look!" Kirsty nudged Rachel as Green Factory's song began. "Courtney has her saxophone!"

The girls were thrilled when Green Factory performed even more wonderfully than they had before. Courtney's saxophone solo sounded perfect, too.

"That's because Sadie's saxophone is back in Fairyland!" Rachel said, as they joined in the applause.

"And our next performance is by Frosty and his Gobolicious Band!" announced the emcee.

Jack Frost and his goblins hurried on stage. As the members of Green Factory passed by, Jack Frost snatched the saxophone from Courtney's hand and passed it to the goblin who had played

earlier. Then Jack Frost grabbed the
microphone and began his rap.

"*I am Jack Frost . . .*" he sang.

But his voice sounded
harsh and whiny, unlike
the deep, cool
sound from the
earlier rap.
The goblin
with the
saxophone was
attempting to
play it, but he
only seemed to
produce strange

honking sounds. Behind them, the other
goblins were trying to sing, clap, and
whistle, but no one could keep the beat.
They sounded terrible!

"They don't have any rhythm at all without the magic saxophone!" Rachel laughed, as the audience members glanced at one another in confusion.

"You're doing it all wrong!" one of the goblins yelled, pulling his neighbor's nose.

"No, you are!" shrieked the other goblin.

Within minutes, the goblins were arguing and wrestling around on the stage. The emcee immediately rushed out, looking frazzled.

"And a big thank you to Frosty and his

Gobolicious Band for their — um —
unique performance!" he mumbled.

"I haven't finished yet!" Jack Frost
snarled, glaring at him.

Two security guards ran out from
the wings and escorted Jack Frost,
complaining loudly, from the stage.
The goblins hurried off, too, still
arguing.

"I don't think Frosty and his Gobolicious
Band will win!" Kirsty giggled.

The girls watched the other two acts,
then waited for the emcee to announce
the results.

"And the first-place prize of a recording
contract with MegaBig Records goes
to . . ." There was a loud drum roll.
"GREEN FACTORY!"

"Hooray, Courtney!" Kirsty cried, as

Green Factory returned to the stage to collect their recording contract from the president of MegaBig Records. "Rachel, isn't it amazing?"

Rachel nodded. "Green Factory really deserves to win," she replied. "And I'm so glad that music everywhere is back to normal again!"

"Me, too," Kirsty agreed. "The world would be awfully dull without music, wouldn't it?"

"And awfully dull without our fairy friends, too!" Rachel winked at Kirsty. "I wonder what our next fairy adventure will be?"

THE SPORTS FAIRIES

Rachel and Kirsty helped all seven Music
Fairies! Now Fairyland and the human
world are in perfect harmony again.

But Jack Frost is always up to new tricks.
This time, he's giving the Sports Fairies
trouble! Can Rachel and Kirsty help

Helena
the Horse-riding
Fairy?

Join their next adventure in this special
sneak peek!

Magic Message

"There," Rachel Walker said, fixing her
hair. "I'm ready. Are you?"

Kirsty Tate buttoned her riding pants
and smiled at her best friend. "Yes," she
said. "I can't wait!"

It was the first day of school vacation,
and Kirsty had come to stay with
Rachel's family for a week. In a few

minutes, they would be setting off for a
riding lesson at the Tippington Stables,
and both girls were looking forward to it.
They always seemed to have the most
fun when they were together — and the
most exciting adventures, too!

Kirsty was just about to open the door,
when something caught her eye.
Rachel's music box was open on her
dresser, even though it had been closed
just a minute before. "Rachel!" she said,
pointing. "Look!"

She and Rachel ran over excitedly.
They had each been given matching
music boxes by the king and queen of
Fairyland, as thank-you presents for
helping the fairies. The two girls had
been friends with the fairies long enough
now to know that the open, tinkling

music box meant only one thing:
Something magical was about to
happen!

Kirsty held her breath as she peeked in
the music box, and then she gasped as
she spotted a piece of paper tucked
inside. As the girls watched, sparkly gold
writing appeared on the paper, letter by
letter.

"It's a message," Rachel whispered, her
heart pounding.

We . . . need . . . your . . . help! the
golden letters spelled.

There's Magic in Every Series!

The Rainbow Fairies

The Weather Fairies

The Jewel Fairies

The Pet Fairies

The Fun Day Fairies

The Petal Fairies

The Dance Fairies

Read them all!

SCHOLASTIC

www.scholastic.com
www.rainbowmagiconline.com

HiT entertainment

RMFAIRY

RAINBOW magic

THE DANCE FAIRIES

They'll Keep You On Your Toes!

▓ SCHOLASTIC

www.scholastic.com
www.rainbowmagiconline.com

HiT entertainment

DANCEF

SPECIAL EDITION

Three Books in One!
More Rainbow Magic Fun!

■SCHOLASTIC

www.scholastic.com
www.rainbowmagiconline.com

HiT entertainment

RMSPECIAL2